At the Back of the North Wind

by

George MacDonald

retold by Dan Larsen

Young Reader's Christian Library

**Illustrated by
Ken Save**

A BARBOUR BOOK

© 1991 by Barbour and Company, Inc.
All Rights Reserved
Printed in the United States of America
ISBN 1-55748-188-1

Typesetting By Typetronix, Inc.
Cape Coral, FL 33904

92 93 94 95 5 4 3 2

Contents

Introduction

"I do not write for children," George Mac-
Donald said, "but for the childlike, whether of
five, or fifty, or seventy-five."

At the Back of the North Wind is for the childlike — those who never lose the child's sense of
wonder and delight and simple faith. First pub-
lished in 1871, the book was very popular for
many years. Then, sadly, it began disappearing
from circulation and was almost unheard of for
some time.

But all good things last. They may go away for
a time, but, like the sun, which sets and then
rises, they will come back. Happily, this story
began to appear in print again. It will probably
never fade away, because the beauty and power it
contains are ageless, and immense.

Come and share the amazing adventures of
Diamond, the little boy who learns the one true
meaning of life.

May we all grow to be like little children
forever.

Dan Larsen

DIAMOND WOKE IN THE MIDDLE OF THE NIGHT

1
The Hay Loft

The little boy, Diamond, woke in the middle of the night. He sat up and listened. The wind was whistling and moaning outside. But there was something else. At least Diamond thought there was.

A voice. Someone had called his name, he was sure. He listened, and there it was again. It was a gentle voice, and yet it seemed a bit angry now. It seemed to be coming from outside.

Diamond wasn't really afraid. But he was curious. The voice seemed to come through a little hole in the wall. The past few nights the north wind had been blowing, and it came in through this hole in Diamond's bedroom sharp and cold. Diamond's mother had pasted a piece of paper over the hole. A corner of the paper had come loose, and now the wind whistled in through the tiny crack. The voice seemed to come in with the wind. Diamond put his ear up to the paper on the hole.

"What do you mean by closing up my window, little boy?" the voice asked, more clearly now.

"What window?" Diamond asked.

"You stuffed hay into it three times last night, and I had to blow it out each time. And now you've covered it with paper."

"You can't mean this little hole! This isn't a window, it's a hole into my bedroom."

"I didn't say it was *a* window. I said it was *my* window."

"But it can't be a window. Windows are to see out of."

"Well, that's just what I made this window

"WHAT WINDOW?" DIAMOND ASKED

for," said the voice.

"But you are outside!" said Diamond. "You don't need a window."

"You say that windows are to see out of. Well, I'm in my house, and I want windows to see out of."

"But you've made a window into my bedroom!"

"Well, your mother has three windows into my dancing room, and you have three into my garret. Now please open my window."

"Well, Mother says I ought to obey, but, you see, the north wind will blow in my face if I do."

"I am the north wind."

Diamond's breath caught. "Oh," he said. He thought for a moment. "Then, will you promise not to blow on my face if I do?"

"I can't promise that," said the voice.

"But you'll give me a toothache. Mother's got it

"I AM THE NORTH WIND"

already.''

"But what's to become of me without a window?"

"I don't know. But it will be worse for me than for you."

"No, it will not, I promise you that. You will be much the better for it. Just believe what I say, and do as I tell you."

"Well, I *can* pull my blankets over my head," said Diamond. He tore off the piece of paper, and at once the cold wind struck him in the chest.

He scrambled to his bed and pulled the covers over his head. But the voice began again. It was much louder now, though it was still very gentle.

"What is your name, little boy?" it asked.

"Diamond."

"What a funny name!"

"It's a very nice name," said Diamond. And to him, it was. Diamond was the name of a great

DIAMOND PULLED THE COVERS OVER HIS HEAD

horse, whose stable was just below the hay loft where little Diamond the boy slept. The horse belonged to little Diamond's father, who was a coachman. Diamond's family lived in a coach house, the horse below, the people above. Diamond's father loved the old horse so much that he named his little boy after him. Diamond the boy was very proud of his name.

"Diamond is a very pretty name," he said, a little crossly.

"A diamond is rather a useless thing, actually," said the voice.

"That's not true!" said Diamond. "Diamond is very nice. Very big, and quiet all night. And he makes a jolly noise in the morning, getting up on his four great legs. It's like thunder."

"You don't seem to know what a diamond is," said the voice.

"Oh, don't I? Diamond is a great and good

DIAMOND'S FAMILY LIVED IN A COACH HOUSE

horse, and he sleeps right under me. He is Old Diamond, and I am Young Diamond. Or if you like, Mr. North Wind, he's Big Diamond, and I'm Little Diamond, and I don't know which of us my father likes best.''

The voice laughed then, a beautiful laugh, very soft and musical. ''I'm not Mr. North Wind,'' the voice said.

''You said you were the north wind,'' said Diamond, still under the covers.

''I didn't say *Mister* North Wind,'' said the voice.

''Well, Mother says I ought to be polite.''

''Then let me tell you that I don't think it at all polite of you to say *Mister* to me. And you can't say it's polite to lie there talking with your head under your covers and never look up to see what kind of person you are talking to. I want you to come out with me.''

"I WANT YOU TO COME OUT WITH ME"

"I want to go to sleep," said Diamond.

"You will sleep all the better tomorrow night," said the voice. "Will you take your head out of the covers?" The voice sounded a little angry again.

"No!" said Diamond.

Just then a blast of wind burst through the cracks between the boards of the wall, snapping one of the boards in two and sweeping the covers off Diamond. Then just as suddenly, it was calm.

Diamond stared up in terror. Leaning over him was a tall, tall woman. She was very pale but very beautiful. Her dark eyes flashed and her dark hair streamed out in every direction, as if the darkness of the hay loft were made of her hair.

Diamond was suddenly no longer afraid. He gazed at the beautiful face. Light seemed to shine out from her eyes and glow all around her face.

LEANING OVER HIM WAS A TALL, TALL WOMAN

"I'm sorry I was forced to be so rough with you," she said. "Will you go with me now, little Diamond?"

"I will. Yes, I will," he said, holding out his arms. "But I should get my clothes."

"Never mind your clothes," she said. "You will not be cold with me. Nobody is cold with the north wind."

"I thought everybody was."

"People are cold only because they are not with the north wind, but without it."

Diamond wasn't old enough yet to wonder if this were a joke. He wasn't old enough to think of himself as too wise to believe her. So he simply believed her. He stretched out his arms to her again.

The lady's face drew back. "Follow me, Diamond," she said.

He got out of his little bed, tucked away in the

HE STRETCHED OUT HIS ARMS TO HER AGAIN

soft hay, and went up to her.

"You're not afraid?" she asked.

"No, ma'am," he said. "But Mother would never let me go out without shoes. She never said anything about clothes, so I don't think she'd mind that."

"I know your mother very well," said the lady. "She is a good woman. I have visited her often. I was with her when you were born. I saw her laugh and cry both at once. I love your mother, Diamond."

"How is it that you didn't know my name, then, ma'am? Please, ma'am, am I to say *ma'am* to you, ma'am?"

"One question at a time, dear boy," she said, laughing. "I knew your name quite well, but I wanted to hear what you would say for it. I know all about you and your mother. Now, will you go with me?"

"YOU'RE NOT AFRAID?" SHE ASKED

"Yes, I will."

"Now for the next question. You're not to call me ma'am. You must call me just my own name — North Wind."

"Well, please, North Wind, I am ready to go with you. You are so beautiful."

"You must not be ready to go with everything beautiful all at once, Diamond."

"But what's beautiful can't be bad," Diamond said. "You're not bad, are you, North Wind?"

"No, I'm not bad. But sometimes beautiful things go bad by doing bad, and it takes some time for their badness to spoil their beauty. So little boys may be mistaken if they go after things because they are beautiful."

"Well, I will go with you because you're beautiful and good too."

"Ah, but there's another thing, Diamond,"

"NORTH WIND... I AM READY TO GO WITH YOU."

the lady said. "What if I should look ugly without being bad? You may see me with my face all black, or flapping wings like a bat's, as big as the whole sky. If you hear me raging ten times worse than the blacksmith's wife or peering into people's windows, you must just believe that I'm doing my work. And if I change into a snake or a tiger, you must not let go of my hand. For my hand will never change in yours if you keep a good hold. If you keep a hold you will know who I am all the time, even if I may look like something awful. Do you understand?"

"Yes," said Diamond, staring into her deep, dark eyes.

"Come along, then," she said, disappearing behind the mound of hay.

Little Diamond, in his nightgown, crept after her.

"IF I CHANGE... YOU MUST NOT LET GO OF MY HAND"

THE HORSE NUZZLED THE BOY WITH HIS BIG VELVETY NOSE

2
North Wind

As Diamond turned the corner of the hay mound, he hesitated for a moment. The stairway ahead was invisible to him. North Wind's long, dark hair spread out behind her as she went down the stairs. But right beside Diamond was the trap door leading down to Diamond the horse's stable. A lantern shone up through the trap door. That way looked inviting, so Diamond climbed down the ladder.

There the horse nuzzled the boy with his big velvety nose, and the boy patted the horse's neck and kissed his great furry cheek. Being a little boy, Diamond soon forget all about North Wind. Soon he was petting the horse and pulling bits of straw from his mane.

This went on for several minutes. Suddenly Diamond remembered. North Wind! She must be waiting for him. He ran out into the yard.

But there was no lady. She was gone. It was a clear night, and the stars were glittering. The air was frosty. Standing in his nightgown, his bare feet on the icy cobblestones of the paved yard, Diamond began shivering.

Maybe she's hiding, he thought. He went around the corner of the stable. But as soon as he rounded the corner, a sharp wind struck him in the chest. He decided to go forward to look in the little garden just off the kitchen. But with each step, the wind seemed to blow stronger. Diamond's teeth began to chatter. After a few more steps, he could go no farther. So he turned his back to the wind and trotted back toward the yard.

Strange! Now that he was going in this direction

THERE WAS NO LADY... SHE WAS GONE!

the wind had dropped. It felt almost warm now as it came gently on his bare calves. Diamond stopped and turned around again, and the wind raged into his face, stinging his eyes and plastering his nightgown against him. He turned his back to the wind again, and the wind became a gentle breeze once more.

This must be North Wind, he thought. She wants me to go this way. Soon he came to a little doorway in a stone wall. This led into the garden of the Colemans. The Coleman family owned a large house and the stables and the coach house where Diamond and his mother and father lived. Diamond's father was the coachman for the Colemans.

Diamond had never been in this garden before. Nor had he ever been outside late at night. He stood in the middle of the lawn, the soft, warm grass under his bare feet, the stars twinkling

HE CAME TO A LITTLE DOORWAY IN A STONE WALL

overhead, and he looked around in wonder. It's like fairyland, he thought.

But where was North Wind? Why had she left him all alone? He began to cry.

Just then the Colemans's maid, Mrs. Crump, walked by a large window facing the garden and saw little Diamond standing in the garden in his nightgown. He must be walking in his sleep, she thought. She rushed into the garden, took him by the hand, and led him inside the house.

She took him to the drawing room, where young Miss Coleman sat by a dressing table, brushing her hair. She stood up as the maid and Diamond entered the room, and her long, dark hair fell to her knees. She was very beautiful. Through his tears Diamond thought she looked just like North Wind. He ran to her with his arms out.

Miss Coleman's heart melted on seeing the little

MRS. CRUMP SAW DIAMOND STANDING IN THE GARDEN

boy rush to her. She dropped to her knees and scooped him into her arms, where he clung, sobbing.

Mrs. Crump took Diamond home a little while later. His mother put him to bed and sat watching him as he slept. She was worried. Her little Diamond had never walked in his sleep before. Was he sick?

As the days passed, Diamond began to wonder if it were all a dream. North Wind? A big, beautiful lady who entered his room as if by magic? His walk in the night? Before a week had passed, he was sure it never happened.

All that week his mother watched him closely. She went into his little loft bedroom several times each night to make sure he was safe in his bed.

The weather was getting colder. Frost covered the grass every morning now. Diamond had to stay inside for a few weeks because his shoes had

SHE SCOOPED HIM INTO HER ARMS

worn out. His mother was saving pennies to buy him a new pair.

One day his mother brought home a new pair of shoes. When he had put them on, his mother let him go outside to play. As he played, he found himself by the little garden door, and at once he remembered his dream. Was it really a dream? Would the garden look the same to him as it did in the dream? Slowly he went through the doorway and out into the soft grass.

Yes, it was the same, but, no, it wasn't. All the flowers were gone, killed by the frosts. Diamond looked around sadly.

There! There was one brave little flower left, a tiny primrose. He ran to it and knelt down. As he watched, a little breeze began gently stirring its leaves. Curious. Diamond could feel no wind. Yet the little flower was stirring gently, as if bowing and saying, How do you do?

...A TINY PRIMROSE!

That night Diamond fell asleep as soon as his mother tucked him in.

Hours later, he woke suddenly and sat up in the darkness.

"Open the window, Diamond," came a voice. It was coming from the same hole in the wall. Diamond's mother had pasted the paper over it again.

"Open the window," came the voice again. "I don't have too much time."

And suddenly it all came back to Diamond. It *wasn't* a dream! Quickly, he scrambled to the hole. "But, North Wind," he said as he picked at the corner of the paper, "what's the use? You left me all alone last time."

"Yes, but that was your fault," she said. "I had work to do. And besides, a gentleman should never keep a lady waiting."

"But I'm not a gentleman," said Diamond,

"OPEN THE WINDOW, DIAMOND"

scratching at the paper. "I'm going to be a coachman, and a coachman is not a gentleman."

"We call your father a gentleman in our house," said North Wind.

"He doesn't call himself one."

"That doesn't matter. Every man ought to be a gentleman, and your father is one."

Diamond was very pleased to hear this. Finally he got the paper off, and the next instant a young girl stood before him.

Diamond's face fell. "Oh, dear!" he said. "Who are you?"

"I'm North Wind," said the girl.

"But you're no bigger than I am!"

"Do you think I care how big or little I am? Didn't you see me this evening? I was much smaller then."

"No. Where were you?"

"Behind the primrose. Didn't you see the leaves

...A YOUNG GIRL STOOD BEFORE HIM

blowing?"

"Yes." Diamond was staring now, his eyes round.

"Hurry, then, if you want to go with me," said North Wind.

"But you're not big enough to take care of me," said Diamond.

"I'm big enough to show you the way anyhow. But if you won't come, then you must stay. I must hurry tonight."

"I'll come! But I have to get dressed first."

"Very well. But hurry! I'll go shake the primrose leaves until you come."

Then Diamond saw a gleam of pale light vanishing down the stairs. Quickly, he dressed himself, crept down the stairs, and ran to the Colemans's garden. There was the girl. Was it really North Wind?

"YOU'RE NOT BIG ENOUGH TO TAKE CARE OF ME!"

She held out her hand. "Come along," she said. Diamond took her hand. Though it was very cold, it was pleasant and it felt full of life. She led him to the garden wall, which was taller than both of them. The girl gave a light leap and stood on the top of the wall, looking down at Diamond.

"Stop, stop!" he cried. "I can't jump like that."

"You didn't try," she said.

"Give me your hand, and I'll try."

She reached down and Diamond took her hand. Then he leaped and suddenly found himself standing next to the girl.

He gasped in delight. "This is nice!" he said.

The girl was taller now and her hair was longer. "Come," she said, and, holding Diamond's hand, leaped again. This time they landed lightly in the road. Now she seemed taller still.

...A LIGHT LEAP AND SHE STOOD ON THE TOP OF THE WALL

NORTH WIND

"I have some unpleasant work to do tonight," she said. "I must do it before I go out to sea. Come!" She began running.

It seemed to Diamond that he wasn't running at all, just gliding along. Yet they were going as fast as the wind. North Wind was growing taller all the time. They turned this way and that, going down narrow streets and alleys, through gardens and backyards, around stone walls, up wide cobblestone streets. Soon they came to a house with the front door open. They went in and down a long hallway until they came to the foot of a stairway and stopped.

Diamond turned to North Wind and staggered backward, gasping in terror!

Instead of North Wind, there stood beside him a huge wolf with gleaming fangs! Its fierce eyes were blazing and staring upstairs. With a deep snarl, it leaped up the stairs.

IT SEEMED TO DIAMOND THAT... HE WAS GLIDING ALONG

Then it seemed that the whole house shook. Windows rattled and there came a great crash from upstairs. Diamond's face was white. North Wind can't be eating one of the children! His little heart pounding, he crept up the stairs.

Suddenly North Wind herself met him, took his hand, and rushed down the stairs and out of the house.

Diamond's heart was still pounding. "I hope you haven't eaten a baby!" he gasped.

North Wind laughed. Her laughter was musical and merry. "No, I didn't eat a baby," she said. "You wouldn't have to ask such a foolish question if you hadn't let go of my hand. You would have seen how I dealt with a nurse who was calling a child bad names and telling her she was wicked. The nurse had been drinking. I saw an ugly gin bottle in the cupboard."

"And you frightened her?" asked Diamond.

"I HOPE YOU HAVEN'T EATEN A BABY!"

"Yes, indeed!" said North Wind, laughing again. "I flew at her throat, and she tumbled over with such a crash that the other servants all ran into the room. She'll be turned out from the house tomorrow, I believe."

"But didn't you frighten the little one?" asked Diamond.

"She never saw me. The woman would not have seen me either if she had not been wicked."

Diamond looked puzzled.

"Good people see good things, and bad people see bad things," said North Wind. "I had to make myself look like a bad thing before she could see me. If I had put on any shape other than a wolf's, she wouldn't have seen me. You see, inside her her own shape is growing to be just that, a wolf."

"I don't know what you mean," said Diamond, "but it's all right. I believe you."

"...SHE TUMBLED OVER WITH SUCH A CRASH!"

They climbed a tall grassy hill now. The stars were bright in the black sky. North Wind was a lady again, very tall, her black hair flowing out all around them. She turned to Diamond. Her eyes seemed to shine like the stars. Diamond gazed into her face and all his fear was gone.

"Now," she said, "whatever you do, don't let go of my hand. I might have lost you the last time, only I was not in too much of a hurry. Now I'm in a hurry."

She looked off toward London, the tiny gas-lights from the houses below them twinkling golden like the stars twinkling silver above them. As they stood there, North Wind began to grow.

HER EYES SEEMED TO SHINE LIKE STARS

"I MUST SWEEP ONE OF MY ROOMS TONIGHT"

3
Out in the Storm

As she grew taller and taller, North Wind began to tremble. Her hair spread out wider and wider like a soft black cloud, until Diamond could no longer see the stars.

"I must sweep one of my rooms tonight," came her huge voice from high in the sky. "Those careless, untidy children make it such a mess."

The next moment she was only a tall lady again. She smiled down at Diamond. "Diamond, I am afraid you might not keep hold of me, so I've made a place for you in my hair. Come." She lifted him over her shoulder and said, "Get in, Diamond."

She had woven a kind of nest in her hair, like a

pouch. Diamond crawled in and grabbed two braids of hair that she had twisted like ropes.

The next instant North Wind was growing again. She grew taller than the tallest trees Diamond had ever seen. Then as he looked down, the ground began dropping away below them. They were flying! Diamond hung on as tight as he could. But soon he discovered that, though his heart was pounding, he felt safe with North Wind.

Below, the houses of London rushed past in a blur. There was a great roaring sound, though on North Wind's back all was calm.

Diamond didn't know whether North Wind could hear him, but he decided to try. "Please, North Wind," he shouted, "what is that sound?"

"My broom," she said, "I am the old woman who sweeps the cobwebs from the sky. Only I'm

THEY WERE FLYING!

busy with the floor now."

They flew in wide circles around and around London. Far below, the dust blew along the streets as in a hurricane. Soon North Wind slowed and dropped down lower, just above the rooftops. The streets were nearly empty. The gas lamps flickered inside their glass covers.

Along one street came a little girl about Diamond's age. She was dressed in tattered, shabby clothes and carried a broom. Or rather the broom was carrying her. It seemed to want to tear itself out of her hands as the wind blew against her. She struggled against the wind, her ragged clothes flapping wildly.

"Oh, please, North Wind, won't you help that little girl?" shouted Diamond.

"No, Diamond," North Wind said, "I must not leave my work. Of course, you can help her if you like."

SHE WAS DRESSED IN TATTERED, SHABBY CLOTHING

"Oh, let me! But will you be able to wait for me?"

"No, I can't wait. You must do it yourself. And, mind, the wind will get hold of you too. And if you go, I cannot promise to take you home, though I can promise you that it will be all right in the end. You will get home somehow."

"Well, I want to help her, no matter what," Diamond said.

And suddenly he was on the street. North Wind was only a tall lady again, but with her hair flying up over the house tops. She stepped back a step and instantly was taller than the houses. Then she was gone, and the wind almost blew Diamond over. A clay chimney pot crashed at his feet.

Just then the little girl flashed by, crying, her legs going as fast as they could as the wind drove her down the street. Diamond ran after her and

"I WANT TO HELP HER... NO MATTER WHAT!"

caught her in his arms. Together they tumbled in the street. And suddenly the girl was laughing instead of crying.

As they sat up, Diamond took the girl by the hand. With his other hand he grabbed a lamp post next to him.

"Where are you going?" Diamond shouted.

"Home," she said, gasping for breath.

"Then I'll go with you and take care of you," he said.

"Where is your sweep crossing?"

"I don't sweep."

"What do you do, then? You ain't big enough for most things."

"I don't know what I do. Nothing, I suppose. My father's Mr. Coleman's coachman."

"You have a father?" she asked, her voice rising.

"WHERE ARE YOU GOING?" DIAMOND SHOUTED

Diamond looked puzzled. "Yes, haven't you?" he asked.

"No, nor mother either," she said, "Old Sal's all I got." Now she began crying again.

"Move on!" shouted a policeman, who had just come up behind them. The wind seemed a bit calmer now.

Holding Diamond's hand, the girl, who was called Nanny, led him to her home. They went down a narrow, dirty alley and Nanny knocked on a cellar door. There was no answer.

"Sal's home but she won't let me in," Nanny said. "She does this whenever I'm out late." She began to cry again. Then she wiped her tears with her frock and took Diamond's hand.

"We'd better go home to my house," said Diamond.

"Where do you live?" Nanny asked.

Diamond looked up and down the narrow street

THEY WENT DOWN A NARROW, DIRTY ALLEY

and at all the dark buildings. He had never been here before. "I don't really know," he said.

"Then you're worse off than I am," she said.

Hand in hand, they wandered down the streets, turning right or left, whichever way seemed to look better. Diamond was sure he was being no help at all, and he began to feel foolish and a little afraid.

He didn't know it, but he *was* helping Nanny. She was much happier with him than she had been alone.

There were fewer and fewer houses along this street. Nanny and Diamond were passing out of the city. To their right was a bare field with some big empty barrels lying in the dry grass. Soon Diamond and Nanny turned off the road into a narrow lane. It went on and on, into the country.

The wind was much calmer now. The lane began climbing a hill. "North Wind must be gone

HE DIDN'T KNOW IT... BUT HE WAS HELPING NANNY

home by now," Diamond said. "I shouldn't have been out so late, but I got down to help you."

Nanny stared at Diamond. "What?" she said.

So Diamond had to tell Nanny the whole story about North Wind and him. Nanny said she didn't believe a word of it.

Just then they reached the top of the hill. Suddenly a blast of wind hit them in the back, and they had to run down the hill as fast as they could. At the bottom of the hill ran a stone wall. They were headed straight toward a wooden door in the wall. They couldn't stop because of the wind, and as Diamond hit the door at a full run, it swung open.

"Ah, ha!" cried Diamond. "North Wind has brought me home to our master's garden. Come in with me, Nanny. Mother will give you some breakfast."

THEY COULDN'T STOP BECAUSE OF THE WIND!

"No, thank you. I must be off. It's nearly morning." She ran up the hill and disappeared over the top.

Diamond ran through the garden to the stable door and climbed up into his loft. And it felt so nice to be in his own little bed again.

IT FELT SO NICE TO BE IN HIS OWN BED AGAIN

...SLIDING DOWN A TULIP WAS A TINY GIRL!

4
The Cathedral

Diamond didn't tell his mother about his adventures with North Wind. He didn't think his mother would mind, if only she knew North Wind. Maybe she did know North Wind. At least North Wind said she knew his mother. Still, his mother might not believe him, as Nanny hadn't. He decided that North Wind would tell him if he was supposed to say anything.

Spring went by, summer came, and yet Diamond hadn't seen North Wind again. One warm evening just before dark, Diamond sat in the Colemans's garden watching some bees among a patch of flowers. Suddenly he heard a tiny voice from the flowers. He bent closer to look. There, sliding down a tulip stem, was a girl no bigger than a dragonfly.

THE CATHEDRAL

"Are you the fairy that herds the bees?" stammered Diamond, staring wide-eyed at the tiny girl.

"I'm not a fairy," she piped.

"You look like one."

"Fairies are much bigger than I am. Besides, a fairy can't grow big and little whenever it wants, even though the nursery tales *do* say so. You silly Diamond, haven't you seen me before?"

As she spoke, a gust of wind bent the tulips over and then was gone.

"North Wind?" Diamond said, still staring hard.

"Must I always be the same size for you to recognize me?" she asked. "Diamond, I cannot stay and chatter. I must get ready. I have to sink a ship tonight."

"Sink a ship! What! With men on it?"

"Yes, and women too."

"How dreadful! I wish you wouldn't talk so."

"NORTHWIND?" DIAMOND ASKED

"It is rather dreadful," she said. "But I have my orders, and I must do it."

"I hope you won't ask me to go with you," Diamond said, his face suddenly pale.

"No, I won't ask you. But you must come, even so."

"I won't, then."

"Won't you?" And suddenly the tiny creature became a tall lady and looked down at Diamond.

He stared up into her eyes. "Please take me," he said. "I know you cannot be cruel."

"No, I couldn't be cruel if I wanted to," she said softly. "I can do nothing cruel, although I often do what looks cruel to those who don't know what I really am doing. The people they say I drown I only carry away to — to — well, to the back of the north wind. That's what they used to call it long ago, although I never have seen the place."

"I COULDN'T BE CRUEL IF I WANTED TO"

"How can you carry them there if you never saw it?"

"I know the way," said North Wind.

"But how is it that you never saw it?"

"Because it is behind me."

"But you can look around."

"Not far enough to see my own back," said North Wind. "No, I always look before me. In fact, I grow quite blind and deaf when I try to see behind me. I only mind my work. It's all the same to me whether I let a bee out of a tulip or sweep the cobwebs from the sky. Anyway, you will go with me tonight?"

"I don't want to see a ship sunk," said Diamond.

"But suppose I had to take you?"

"Then of course I must go."

"There's a good Diamond! Only you must go to bed first. That's the law about children. I

"I DON'T WANT TO SEE A SHIP SUNK"

can't take you till you're in bed. Besides, I have much to do to get everything ready."

And suddenly she was gone.

When Diamond went home, his mother looked at him and stopped what she was doing at the stove. "You don't look very well, Diamond," she said. She came to him, knelt down, and took his face gently in her hands.

"I feel well," said Diamond.

"Well, I think you had better go to bed," she said.

"All right, Mother."

She continued to stare up at the loft opening for several moments after Diamond had climbed up.

Diamond woke suddenly to the sound of a great rumbling in the sky, like giant bass drums echoing through a hugh metal vault. In a moment Diamond realized it was thunder. Then he heard a voice. "Come up, Diamond. It's all

"YOU DON'T LOOK VERY WELL, DIAMOND"

ready. I'm waiting for you."

The tiles of the roof were shifted aside and a gigantic but very lovely arm reached down to Diamond. He put his hand in the huge palm and it closed gently on his arm. Suddenly he was being lifted up through the roof. Outside the sky was chaos. Lightning crackled, the wind howled, and thick black clouds shifted heavily.

North Wind was now only a tall lady again, cradling Diamond in her arms. "I'm afraid you will feel the wind in front of me, Diamond," she said. "You had better climb into my hair."

"I don't mind," he said. "It's so nice to feel your arms around me."

"Well, then, I'll keep you in front. I'll need only one arm to take care of you, though I'll need the other to sink the ship."

Diamond shuddered. "Then you do mean to sink the ship?"

A GIGANTIC BUT VERY LOVELY ARM REACHED DOWN

"Yes," she said.

"How can you take care of a poor little boy with one arm and sink a ship with the other? It's not like you."

"What am I like, Diamond?"

"The kindest, goodest, best person in the world," he said, clinging tighter to her.

"Why am I good to you?" she asked. "Have you ever done anything for me?"

"No," he said.

"Then I must be good to you because I choose to be good to you?"

"Yes."

"That's it. I am good to you because I like to be good."

"But why shouldn't you be as good to other people as you are to me?"

"But I am, Diamond."

"But how can that be?"

"You say the arm that holds you is good. Do

"THE KINDEST, GOODEST, BEST PERSON IN THE WORLD!"

you think the other arm I sink a ship with is bad? Don't you think the part of me that you don't know must be as good as the part of me that you do know?"

"Yes, it must be," Diamond said. "But it doesn't seem good to me."

"That's another matter," said North Wind. "It may not seem so to you. I will just tell you that it is so, and you must just believe me."

Diamond snuggled closer to North Wind. "I do believe you," he said. "But I won't like to see the ship sunk, you know."

"And that's another matter too," she said, smiling, "Doing something is not always the same as liking it."

North Wind rose into the sky. Her hair flew out all around her, seeming to fall all the way to the ground, far below. "I am going to let you rest in a special place while I do my work," came

NORTHWIND ROSE INTO THE SKY

her great voice. "I will come back for you."

They were among the storm clouds. The wind stung into Diamond's face. He couldn't tell which was North Wind's hair and which were clouds writhing past them. All was black. In the bursts of white light from the flashes of lightning Diamond could see the tiny whitecaps of the black sea far, far below.

Soon they came to a grassy hill rising up from the seashore. Just ahead in the gloom stood a tall, gray stone cathedral.

"What's that?" cried Diamond.

"A very good place for you to wait," said North Wind. She settled down gently on the roof and went through an open doorway into a tall tower. Inside she set Diamond on his feet. They stood at the top of a stone stairway that twisted away below them into the blackness. Diamond reached up for North Wind's hand. She took it

AHEAD IN THE GLOOM STOOD A TALL, GRAYSTONE CATHEDRAL

and led him down and down and around and around, then opened a door and went out into a narrow balcony that ran around the wall of the central part of the church. The balcony had no railing.

Diamond gasped and clutched North Wind's hand.

"Why are you trembling, little Diamond?" she asked.

"It's so deep down below," he said, "I — I'm afraid."

"It is rather deep," she said. "But you were a hundred times higher out in the sky just a moment ago."

"Yes, but somebody's arm was about me then."

"Such nonsense you talk! Don't you know I've got a hold of you?"

"Yes, but somehow I can't feel comfortable."

THE BALCONY HAD NO RAILING!

"If you were to fall, I would be down after you and catch you before a watch could tick," she said.

"I still don't like it, though," he said. And the next instant he was screaming, "Oh, oh, oh!" because suddenly North Wind had let go of his hand and disappeared in the darkness. He crouched low on the ledge, shaking. He heard her voice somewhere ahead. "Come after me."

But he couldn't move. The next moment he felt a gentle, cool breeze on his face, blowing on him in little puffs. With each puff Diamond felt his faintness blowing away, and his fear with it. Soon he stood up. The little puffs kept blowing in his face. Now he began walking, then marching steadily. His fear was gone. His little steps echoed hugely in the gaping stone chasm below.

He came to a little wooden door and went down another stairway. At the bottom stood

HE BEGAN WALKING...THEN MARCHING... HIS FEAR GONE!

North Wind. She held him close, kissing him on the forehead.

"Why did you leave me?" Diamond asked.

"Because I wanted you to walk alone," she said.

"But the wind is what made me brave."

"Yes, I know. You had to be taught courage. And you couldn't know what it was without feeling it. But don't you think you would try to be brave yourself next time?"

"Yes, I do," he said. "But trying isn't much."

"Yes, it is, a great deal, for it's a beginning. And a beginning is the greatest thing of all. Now I must be going. I will be back for you, and you will be home before morning."

And she was gone.

Now Diamond looked around him. High above on the walls were great stained-glass windows. The moon had risen, peering out now and then

"TRYING IS A GREAT DEAL....FOR IT'S A BEGINNING"

from behind the storm clouds. In the moonlight the faces of the Apostles in the windows seemed to come to life. They stared down at Diamond, their bright, piercing eyes following him as he slowly walked down the aisle of the cathedral. The room was so huge! Even his little footsteps boomed like thunder. Toward the front Diamond came upon a thick, musty-smelling rug. He sat down on this, staring up at the Apostles. Finally he lay down and before long closed his eyes.

He must have slept, because suddenly he woke. Or at least he thought he did. The moon had risen higher, the clouds had passed, and the pale light streamed in through the windows. Diamond thought he heard voices, whisperings. They were coming from high up, in the windows. The Apostles were whispering to one another!

"What do you think, Matthew," came a whisper as deep and huge as the cathedral itself, "do

HE SAT DOWN...STARING UP AT THE APOSTLES

you think North Wind is up to her old tricks again?"

"It must be, Peter," came another voice. "I wonder if she means to leave the little boy here all night."

"Someone really should do something about her," came a third voice. "She can't expect *us* to watch him all night. As if we had nothing better to do!"

Now Diamond was angry. He meant to stand up and shout at the Apostles, telling them they had no right to talk about North Wind like that. But, strangely, he found that he was still lying down and that his eyes were closed. He struggled to open his eyes and sit up. He must have been dreaming after all. No! There were the voices again. But try as he might, Diamond could not open his eyes. He heard the voices fading, fading, fading. . . .

"SHE CAN'T EXPECT US TO WATCH HIM ALL NIGHT!"

"...I THINK HE LOOKS PRETTY BOBBISH"

5
The Journey

Diamond woke and sat up. He was in his own little room in the loft. Morning sunlight reached in through cracks in the boards of the walls. Then he remembered his dream. Or was it a dream? If he were at the cathedral, how did he get home again? Well, North Wind must have come for him, he guessed. And she must have carried him home asleep.

At breakfast that morning Diamond's mother looked at him closely. "I don't think the boy is looking well, husband," she said.

"Don't you?" his father said. "Well, I don't know, I think he looks pretty bobbish. How do you feel yourself, Diamond, my boy?"

"Fine, Father," Diamond said. "At least, I think I've got a little headache."

"There, I told you," said his father and mother at once. And then they both laughed.

His mother sat down at the table, still looking at Diamond. "I've got a letter from my sister at Sandwich," she said. "She wants Diamond to visit her for a while. I think I would like to go too."

"Well, it's fine with me," said his father, smiling.

So a few days later Diamond and his mother went to the little village of Sandwich. Diamond loved to walk down the streets staring at all the quaint old shops and houses. Years ago Sandwich had been a busy seaport, but the sea trade began passing it by for other, bigger ports. Now it was a sleepy little place.

But Diamond's mother had been right about him. He didn't feel well, and he began to tire very easily. On the third day at his aunt's his

"SHE WANTS DIAMOND TO VISIT HER FOR A WHILE"

head ached so much that he had to stay in bed.

He woke that night. The lattice window of his room was open and the curtains were blowing gently. And there was North Wind's beautiful face smiling into his own as she bent over his bed.

"Quick, Diamond," she said. "We must go on a journey."

"Where?" he asked, yawning.

"To a very special place," she said, "I have found a chance to take you there."

"But I'm not well," he said.

"I know that, but you will be better with a little fresh air. And you will have plenty of that."

Diamond climbed out of bed. As soon as he was in her arms, he felt better.

"We must hurry before your aunt comes," North Wind whispered. She stepped through the open window and glided up into the starry sky.

"QUICK DIAMOND... WE MUST GO ON A JOURNEY"

In a moment they were out over the sea.

"I have found a ship sailing north," North Wind said. "I am going to put you in it. You see, Diamond, it is hard for me to get you to this place, because it lies in the very north itself, and of course I can't blow northward."

"But how can you ever get home then?" he asked.

"You are quite right. That is my home, Diamond, though I can never get farther than the front door. I am nobody there, Diamond."

"I'm very sorry," he said.

"Oh, you dear little man, you will be very glad someday to be nobody yourself. But you can't understand that now. Someday you will. But here we are, below. There's your boat. It's not really a boat, of course. It's a yacht of two hundred tons, and the captain is a friend of mine. I am going to put you down there, in the hold.

"THERE'S YOUR BOAT"

That's where they keep spare sails. It will be dark in there, but dry and warm and safe. You can go to sleep there. You must not worry. The yacht shall be my cradle, and you shall be my baby.''

In a moment they were on deck. Diamond heard North Wind lifting a hatch cover, and then he was down below. The canvas sails smelled sweet and oily.

Soon Diamond fell asleep to the gentle rocking of the ship. How long this lasted he couldn't tell. But it seemed to be only a few hours, though it was actually three days.

On the third day the hatch suddenly opened and sunlight poured in. North Wind's arm reached down and lifted Diamond up on deck. The sky and the sea were deep blue here. Giant blocks of ice floated all around the ship. To one of these blocks North Wind leaped, carrying Diamond. She glided down a steep, craggy slope of

NORTHWIND LEAPED, CARRYING DIAMOND

the iceberg and landed on a wide, smooth ledge. In the ice wall was a cave. It looked blue against the blinding white of the wall.

Now Diamond looked at North Wind. Her face was very pale, and she looked worn and tired.

"What's wrong, North Wind?" Diamond cried.

"Nothing much," she said. "I feel faint. But you mustn't mind it. I can bear it quite well."

As she spoke she seemed to be fading away. "I am going, Diamond. I will be all right again soon. You must not be afraid. Just go straight on and you will find me on the doorstep."

Then she disappeared slowly, like smoke. Diamond felt like crying. But she had told him not to fear. And she was always right he knew. Still, he did cry, but only a little.

He stayed in the ice cave for several days as the iceberg floated northward. The sky was so blue

SHE DISAPPEARED SLOWLY... LIKE SMOKE

here it seemed almost too bright to look at for long, like the sun. It was strange, Diamond thought, but all this time he never felt hungry.

One day in his cave he felt his iceberg lurch to a stop. He ran out onto the shelf and saw that he had come to land. Just ahead were jagged, snow-covered mountains that rose up so tall that Diamond had to look almost straight up, bending over backward, to see the peaks. The iceberg was butted up against a great flat rock.

"She said she would be straight ahead," said Diamond to himself. "This must be the place." He could reach the rock with only a short leap.

He found a narrow, stony path that wound up into the mountain. After a little while it went into a small valley cut into the side of the slope. The floor of this valley was a long sheet of ice. At the far end a sharp ridge of rock and ice stretched across the width of the valley. In the middle of

"THIS MUST BE THE PLACE"

this ridge was a gap. Just before this gap was what looked like a person sitting. As Diamond came closer and closer he saw who it was.

"North Wind!" he cried. "At her doorstep." He ran up to her. But suddenly he stopped and stared. Her face was as white as the snow, her eyes as blue as the air. She sat very still, her arms drooping. She was staring ahead but didn't seem to see Diamond.

Finally, his voice trembling, Diamond said, "North Wind?"

"Well, child?" she said faintly, her lips hardly moving.

"Are you ill, North Wind?"

"No. I am waiting."

"What for?"

"Until I'm wanted."

"You don't care for me anymore," said Diamond, about to cry.

"ARE YOU ILL, NORTHWIND?"

"Yes, I do," she said. "Only I can't show it. All my love is down at the bottom of my heart. But I feel it bubbling there."

"What do you want me to do next?"

"What do you want to do yourself?"

"To go into the country at your back."

"Then you must go through me."

"I don't know what you mean."

"I mean just what I say. You must walk on as if I were an open door and go right through me."

"But that will hurt you!" Diamond said.

"Not in the least," she said. "It will hurt you, though."

"I don't mind that, if you tell me to do it."

"Do it," she said, very faintly.

Diamond stepped up to her and put out his hand. He could touch nothing. His heart pounding, he walked on. Suddenly the cold stabbed into him. All around him was nothing but blinding

HE COULD TOUCH NOTHING

whiteness. He stumbled ahead, gasping in pain from the cold. A few clumsy steps more and his legs wouldn't move. Then he was falling forward, feeling nothing, falling, falling, falling.

He woke and sat up. The cold was gone. He was lying in a meadow of soft, sweet-smelling grass, full of bright red and yellow flowers. A little stream flowed softly through the meadow. Its bed was not pebbles or mud, but only the meadow grass, which wafted gently in the slow current.

Nearby were trees, tall and thick and deep green. The leaves were so full that Diamond could see no branches. A gentle breeze stirred the trees and the meadow grass. As Diamond stood up he felt the breeze on his face. It was neither warm nor cold. It felt just right, he thought.

He could see no sun in the sky, yet there was bright, golden light. As Diamond slowly wandered along the stream he began to hear, or to

A FEW CLUMSY STEPS MORE AND HIS LEGS WOULDN'T MOVE

think he heard, a quiet, peaceful song from somewhere. He stood still for awhile, listening. The music seemed to come from the stream as it ran glistening and bubbling along. But as he stood listening it seemed that he wasn't hearing the song with his ears but in his head, as if he were dreaming. He thought he could hear words, but he wasn't sure what they were. There was something very soothing about the song.

He stayed here for many days, wandering among the trees, sitting by the stream, or lying in the meadow grass. Day by day, he began to hum softly to himself. He didn't know the songs he hummed, but they seemed to be the ones that the stream sang.

There were other people here. They would smile when they met Diamond, but no one spoke. Everyone seemed to be at peace, very content. Yet there was something else in their faces,

THE MUSIC SEEMED TO COME FROM THE STREAM

Diamond thought. Not sadness, exactly. But not gladness, either. Some kind of longing, perhaps. Or remembering.

Then one day *he* remembered. North Wind! And his mother! And home!

HE REMEMBERED! NORTHWIND... HIS MOTHER... HOME!

"OH DIAMOND... YOU HAVE BEEN SO ILL!"

6
The Seaside

Diamond opened his eyes. The face above him looked familiar. North Wind? No, his mother! There were tears in her eyes. He tried to sit up and throw his arms around her, but he could barely move. He felt very weak.

His mother scooped him up in her arms, shaking with sobs. "Oh, Diamond, my darling, you have been *so* ill," she said.

"No, Mother," he said. "I've only been to the back of the north wind."

"I thought you were dead!" she said, clutching him tightly.

"Oh, there, we're better today, I see," came a man's voice.

Diamond looked up to see the village doctor walk into the room, smiling broadly.

THE SEASIDE

The doctor then spoke to Diamond's mother quietly, telling her she should let Diamond rest. She kissed Diamond, then left the room.

Diamond lay there looking around the room. It seemed so long ago that he had been here. The days at the back of the north wind seemed to go on and on and on. Now that he was back at his aunt's he felt very weak and very hungry. As he lay here he remembered how he came back.

While in the place at the back of the north wind, he had found a tall tree with wide, spreading branches. He noticed that the people there often climbed the tree and sat in its branches for hours. One day he climbed it too and discovered to his delight that from up there he could see anything he wanted — his home, his father, his mother at his aunt's. One afternoon as he sat looking, he saw North Wind, sitting just as he remembered her, very still, very pale. Just then he

ONE DAY... HE CLIMBED IT TOO

knew he wanted to go back to his mother and his home. He scrambled down the tree. As soon as he reached the bottom, he found himself on the ice in front of North Wind. He went up to her, took her ice-cold hand, and called her name.

At the sound of his voice, she slowly took him into her arms. Diamond could feel her coldness go all through him, making him ache deep down inside. Then gradually she began to warm, until she was herself again. She stood up with him in her arms, laughing, and said, "Now we must hurry, for I have my orders and must get to my work."

And then he woke in his room at his aunt's.

Diamond had to stay in bed for a few more days. He slowly recovered his strength. During this time Diamond's mother got a letter from his father. The Colemans had lost all their money and had to sell everything — the house, the stable

HE WENT UP TO HER ... AND CALLED HER NAME

and coach house, the horse, the cart. Now Diamond's father had no job and the family had no home. Could they stay in Sandwich while he looked for another job and home? Father asked in the letter.

"You stay as long as you like, my dears," Diamond's aunt said. But now Diamond's mother had even more to worry about.

One day when Diamond was well enough his uncle drove his mother and him in a pony cart down to the seashore. There he left them for a few hours while he did some business in the village. The fresh sea air would be good for Diamond, his aunt said.

Diamond and his mother sat in the dry grass on a knoll above the beach and looked out over the sand and the sparkling ocean. Here and there a gull cried overhead. There was nothing to be seen in either direction except the sand, the sea, and the blue sky.

DIAMOND AND HIS MOTHER SAT IN THE DRY GRASS

"Oh, dear," Diamond's mother sighed. She wrapped a woolen blanket tighter around Diamond's shoulders. "It's a sad world!"

"Is it?" Diamond asked. "Oh, I didn't know."

"How should you know, child? You've been too well taken care of, I suppose."

"Oh, yes, I have," said Diamond. "I'm so sorry, but I thought you were taken care of too. I thought my father took care of you. I will ask him about it. I think he only must have forgotten."

"Dear boy!" said his mother, smiling now. "Your father's the best man in the world."

"Just as I thought!" said Diamond. "I was sure of it. Well, then, doesn't he take very good care of you?"

His mother's mouth quivered. "Yes, yes, he does," she said. She started to cry now. "But who's to take care of him? And how is he to take care of us if he's got nothing to eat himself?"

SHE STARTED TO CRY

"Oh, dear!" said Diamond. "Hasn't he got anything to eat? Oh, I must go home to him!"

"No, no, child!" said his mother. "He's not come to that yet. But what's to become of us I don't know."

"Are you very hungry, Mother? There's the basket. I thought you put something to eat in it."

"Oh, you silly darling," she said, smiling through her tears. "I didn't say I was hungry."

"Then I don't understand you. Tell me what's the matter."

"There *are* people in the world who have nothing to eat, Diamond."

"Then I suppose they — what do you call it? — die, don't they?"

"Yes, they do," she said gravely. "How would you like that?"

"I don't know. I never tried. But I suppose they go where they get something to eat."

"THEN I SUPPOSE THEY....DIE...DON'T THEY?"

"Probably enough that they don't want it."

"Then that's all right."

"Oh, poor boy. How little you know about things! Mr. Coleman's lost all his money, and your father has nothing to do, and we shall have nothing to eat soon."

"Are you sure, Mother?"

"No, thank heaven, I'm not *sure* of it." She looked down at her lap. "I hope not," she said quietly.

"Then I don't understand. There's a piece of gingerbread in the basket, I know," he said.

"Oh, you little bird! You have no more sense than a sparrow that picks what it wants and never thinks of the winter and the frost and the snow."

"Oh. But the birds get through the winter, don't they?"

"Some of them fall dead on the ground."

SHE LOOKED DOWN AT HER LAP..."I HOPE NOT."

"They must die sometime," Diamond said. He cocked his head and thought for a moment. "They wouldn't like to be birds always. Would you, Mother?"

"What a child you are!" she said.

"Oh, now I remember," said Diamond. "Father told me that day I went to Epping Forest with him that the rose bushes and may bushes and holly bushes were the birds's barns, all ready for the winter."

"Yes, that's true," she said, wiping her tears. "So you see, the birds are provided for. But there are no such barns for you and me, Diamond. We've got to work for our bread."

"Then let's go and work," Diamond said happily, starting to get up. His mother took his arm and pulled him back down beside her, hugging him.

"It's no use," she said. "We don't have anything to do."

HIS MOTHER TOOK HIS ARM AND PULLED HIM BACK

"Then let's wait," he said, smiling up at her.

"Then we'll starve."

"No, there's the basket. Do you know, Mother, I think I'll call that basket the barn."

"It's not a very big barn. And when it's empty, where are we then?"

"At Auntie's cupboard."

"But we can't eat Auntie's things all up and leave her to starve."

"No, no. We'll go back to Father before that. He'll have found a cupboard somewhere by that time."

"How do you know that?" she asked.

"I don't know it," he said. "But *I* don't have a cupboard, and I've always had plenty to eat."

"But that's because I've had a cupboard for you, child."

"And when yours was empty, Auntie opened hers."

"I'VE ALWAYS HAD PLENTY TO EAT"

His mother sighed heavily. "But that can't go on!"

"How do you know?" Diamond asked. "I think there must be a big cupboard somewhere that fills all the little cupboards."

"Well, I wish I could find the door of that cupboard," she said, shaking her heard slowly. But just then she fell silent and looked up, staring out across the sea. She was silent for a long time, thinking. Something she had heard at church just yesterday came to her now, something to do with not worrying about tomorrow, for tomorrow would take care of itself. And something to do with the birds of the air and the lilies in the field, and about our heavenly Father, who feeds us.

Slowly she rose and opened the picnic basket. She looked into her little son's face for several moments, yet her eyes still seemed to be staring far away. Then she smiled and said, quietly, "Let's eat,

SHE WAS SILENT FOR A LONG TIME...THINKING

Diamond."

While they sat eating, Diamond saw something white on the beach, fluttering in the breeze. His mother went to pick it up for him. "It's a book," she said. "It looks like nursery rhymes."

"Oh, please read some!" cried Diamond.

She turned the pages, looking for one that looked good. But every time she turned the pages, a sharp little wind blew them back to the same rhyme. So finally, frustrated, she decided to read that one.

"I know a river," she began, "whose waters run asleep, run run ever singing in the shallows, dumb in the hollow, sleeping so deep, and all the swallows that dip their feathers in the hollows or in the shallows are the merriest swallows of all . . ."

She read on and on. The rhyme never stopped. Diamond snuggled into his blanket in the sand,

"IT'S A BOOK ... IT LOOKS LIKE NURSERY RHYMES"

smiling, a faraway look in his eyes.

"It's all in the wind that blows from behind," continued his mother, "and all in the river that flows forever and all in the grasses and the white daisies and the merry sheep awake or asleep and the happy swallows skimming the shallows and it's all in the wind that blows from behind . . ."

"Why don't you go on, Mother?" said Diamond.

"It's such nonsense!" she said. "I believe it would go on forever."

"That's just what it did," Diamond said.

"What did?"

"The river. That's almost the same tune it sang at the back of the north wind."

His mother let the book fall into her lap. She stared hard at Diamond, her mouth open, and deep worry in her eyes.

SHE STARED HARD AT DIAMOND

HIS FATHER HAD TO DRIVE INTO LONDON EVERYDAY

7
The Mews

Soon Diamond's mother got another letter from his father. His father had been able to buy old Diamond the horse and a four-wheeled cab. And he had found a new place to live, a room over a stable called The Mews. Diamond and his mother could come home now.

But their new place was even smaller than their old one. It had only one main room, plus a very small one for Diamond to sleep in. And there was no garden for Diamond to play in here, only a stone-paved yard where other coachmen rigged their horses and cabs.

Now his father had to drive into London every day and park along the curbs, hoping to get enough customers to make a living. These days were not happy ones for Diamond's mother and father. They could never be sure of having enough money to buy food. And their home was so small and so dismal, compared with the bright, cheery rooms they had had at the Colemans's coach house.

Diamond was recovered now from his illness. At least he seemed okay. His father began taking Diamond with him on his cab runs in the city. He taught Diamond how to harness up the horse and how to drive the cab. Diamond was very proud to be with his father in his father's very own cab, with his very own horse, their beloved old Diamond.

It was during this time that Diamond's mother had another baby, a baby brother for Diamond. Now Diamond's mother was busier than ever with a new baby to take care of. Right away Diamond saw how he could help her. He would sit with the baby on his lap, talking to him and making him laugh, while his mother was busy with

ANOTHER BABY...DIAMOND'S NEW BROTHER

her work. If the baby cried in his crib, Diamond would pick him up and bounce him on his knee.

And Diamond found many other things to do — sweeping the hearth, toasting bread, feeding baby his bottle.

One morning Diamond was playing with the baby while his mother stepped outside to talk with his father. Diamond began to sing to the baby.

"Baby's asleeping, wake up, baby, for all the swallows are the merriest of fellows and have the yellowest children who would go sleeping and snore like a baby disturbing his mother and father and brother and all aboring their ears with his snoring . . ."

Diamond's mother stopped just outside the door, listening to Diamond's song. He went on and on, while the baby cooed in delight.

". . . and Father's the best of all the swallows that build their nest out of the shining shallows

SHE STOPPED JUST OUTSIDE THE DOOR... LISTENING

and he has the merriest children that's baby and Diamond and Diamond and baby and baby and Diamond . . ."

His mother came into the room now. She looked at Diamond with tears in her eyes. Then she bent down, gave him a kiss, and gently took the baby. "Run along to your father, Diamond, dear," she said. "You can ride on the cab with him today. You're such a help to your mother! One would think you'd been among the fairies."

She stood in the doorway with the baby in her arms, gazing at Diamond as he scrambled up into his father's cab.

Downtown, Diamond and his father had only two customers that morning. It was time for lunch, and Diamond's father had parked the cab at the curb while he went into a little shop to buy some bread. Diamond stayed up on the cab box.

Just then a little girl in tattered clothing was

DIAMOND STAYED UP ON THE CAB BOX

sweeping her street crossing when suddenly three boys ran up to her and grabbed her broom.

"Stop it!" she cried, tugging on the broom. "Leave me alone!"

The boys laughed and began calling her names.

Quickly, Diamond climbed down and ran to the girl. He grabbed the broom and helped her pull. The boys began tugging harder. Then one of them let go of the broom and punched Diamond right in the face. The blood ran down from Diamond's nose, but he did not let go.

Just then Diamond's father came out of the shop. "Hey!" he bellowed. Suddenly he was among the boys. His great arm swatted them like flies, sending them sprawling in the street. Then Diamond's father nodded to the little girl and picked up Diamond and carried him to the cab. He carefully wiped Diamond's nose with a handkerchief.

ONE OF THEM...PUNCHED DIAMOND RIGHT IN THE FACE

"I couldn't let them behave that way to a girl, could I, Father?" said Diamond.

His father smiled. "Certainly not, Diamond," he said. Just as North Wind had said, Diamond's father was a gentleman. He was very proud of Diamond.

As they were about to pull away from the curb, the little girl came running up. "Mister," she called. "There's two ladies here that be wantin' a ride."

Suddenly Diamond recognized the little girl. "Nanny!" he called. She smiled at him, gave a little curtsey, and ran off.

Diamond's father stepped down to help the ladies into the cab. "Oh, Mrs. Coleman, Miss Coleman," he said, sweeping off his cap.

"Why, Joseph, can it be you?" said Mrs. Coleman.

"Yes, ma'am," he said, bowing.

DIAMOND RECOGNIZED THE LITTLE GIRL... "NANNY!"

"I see you've got your own cab now," she said. "Who would have thought things would turn out this way? We live in town now, you know. It's not very often we can afford to have a cab. I do hope you and your family are getting along well."

"It is different, to be sure, ma'am. But we're getting along all right."

Then Miss Coleman, who had become very fond of little Diamond, saw him sitting on the cab box. "Oh, I see you've got both your Diamonds with you," she said to his father, and she smiled at Diamond.

"He'll be fit to drive himself before long," Diamond's father said.

"Well, then, you must come and see us, now that you'll know where we live."

Then Diamond's father helped the ladies into the cab and drove them to the address Mrs. Coleman gave him.

"HE'LL BE FIT TO DRIVE HIMSELF BEFORE LONG"

Diamond didn't know it, but the ship North Wind had sunk belonged to Mr. Coleman. It was his last merchant ship. North Wind had been sent to sink the ship so that Mr. Coleman might have one last chance to become an honest man. For years he had been growing richer and richer. But, sadly, he had also been growing more and more dishonest. Now that he had only a small home and a modest place of business in the city he seemed to be growing more honest and humble every day.

That night at supper Diamond's father told his mother about meeting the Coleman ladies.

"Poor dears!" said his mother. "It's worse for them than it is for us. They've been used to such grand things, and for them to come down to a little poky house like that — it breaks my heart to think of it."

"I wonder if Mrs. Coleman has bells on her

THE SHIP NORTHWIND HAD SUNK BELONGED TO MR. COLEMAN

toes," said Diamond, looking dreamily at the ceiling.

His father and mother stared at him. His father looked amused, his mother startled.

"What do you mean, child?" asked his mother, her brows knit.

"She has rings on her fingers, anyhow," said Diamond.

"Of course she has," said his mother. "As any lady would. What has that to do with it?"

"When we were at Sandwich, you said you would have to sell your mother's ring now that we were poor."

"Bless the child, he forgets nothing!" she said. "Really, Diamond, a person has to mind what he says to you. Anyway, Mrs. Coleman is none so poor as all that. No, thank heaven, she's not come to that."

"Is it *really* bad to be poor?" Diamond asked.

"IS IT REALLY BAD TO BE POOR?" DIAMOND ASKED

His mother didn't answer. Her mouth opened to speak, but no words came out. She stared at Diamond for several moments, then looked down at her hands folded in her lap.

Diamond's father took his wife's hand and smiled at her as she looked up at him. Then she smiled too, slowly, sadly. She looked at Diamond. How could a child be so . . .? Where did he get his notions? How was it that he came to say these things? It was so . . . so . . . what was it?

She didn't know, of course, that Diamond had been to the back of the north wind.

DIAMOND'S FATHER TOOK HIS WIFE'S HAND

THE COACHMEN BICKERED OVER DIAMOND

8
A New Friend

Diamond quickly became a favorite among the other coachmen who lived at The Mews. At first they thought he was strange, always so happy and always so helpful and kind. But soon they began to notice that, far from being foolish, he had a sound mind. His questions, and his answers to theirs, were very thoughtful. No, he wasn't crazy, they decided. He was just good.

Most mornings now would find a group of noisy but good-natured coachmen bickering over who would get to have Diamond ride with him that day — that is, when his mother could spare him herself.

One morning Diamond went with his father. They parked the cab at their usual spot. It was slow that morning. Diamond's father began reading a newspaper, sitting on the cab box. Diamond climbed down to take a little walk, as he often did on slow mornings like this.

Soon he came to Nanny's crossing. There she was with her broom. A tall gentleman came up to her just then and gave her a penny. She smiled and curtsied.

"Where do you live, my child?" he asked.

"Paradise Row," she said. "Down in the Area. I live with my wicked old granny."

The gentleman's brows creased. "You shouldn't call your granny wicked," he said.

"But she is," said Nanny, looking up at him with wide eyes. "If you don't believe me, you can come and take a look at her."

"Hmmm," said the man. "still, you shouldn't say so."

"I shouldn't? Everybody calls her wicked old granny, even them that's as wicked as her. You

"YOU SHOULDN'T CALL YOUR GRANNY WICKED"

should hear her swear. There's nothing else like it in the Row!" She looked proud.

The gentleman was looking down at the street. What a shame, he thought, such a nice little girl in such bad keeping.

"Please, sir," said Diamond, "her granny's very cruel to her sometimes and shuts her out in the streets at night when she's late."

"Is this your brother?" the man asked Nanny.

"No, sir," she said.

"How does he know your granny, then? He doesn't look like one of her sort."

"Oh, no, sir. He's a good boy. He's quite . . ." She tapped her forehead with a finger and rolled her eyes. Then she stepped up to the man and whispered, "The cabbies call him God's baby. He's not quite right in the head, you know."

The man nodded. Then he turned to Diamond. The quiet sweetness of Diamond's face did indeed

"HE'S NOT QUITE RIGHT IN THE HEAD, YOU KNOW"

seem silly, the man thought. He decided to say something to Diamond to be nice.

"Well, my little man," he said, "and what can you do?"

"Drive a cab," said Diamond.

"Good! And what else?"

"Nurse a baby, clean Father's boots, and make him a bit of toast for his tea. I can curry a horse, but only if somebody puts me on its back, so I don't count that."

The man was smiling now. "Can you read?" he asked.

"No, but Mother can and Father can," said Diamond. "And they're going to teach me some-day soon."

"Well, here's a penny for you. When you can read, come and see me and I'll give you sixpence and a book with pictures in it."

"DRIVE A CAB", SAID DIAMOND

"Please, sir, where am I to come?" asked Diamond.

Not quite right, indeed, thought the man. You're no silly, my boy. No silly at all. He handed Diamond a card. "This will tell you where I live," he said. Then he said good-bye to them and walked across the street.

On the sidewalk he turned and saw Diamond give his penny to the girl. "Here," Diamond said. "You may have mine. I've got a father and mother and a little brother, and you've got nothing but a wicked old granny."

The gentleman smiled to himself as he continued on his way.

Back on the cab Diamond showed his father the gentleman's card. "A Mr. Raymond," his father read. "Why, the address is only a few blocks down from The Mews." He handed Diamond the card. "Take care of it, my boy, for it may lead to

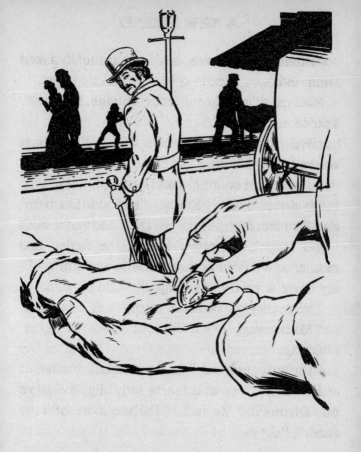

HE SAW DIAMOND GIVE HIS PENNY TO THE GIRL

something. God knows, in these hard times a man wants as many friends as he's ever likely to get."

"Haven't you got friends enough, Father?" asked Diamond.

"Well, I've no right to complain. But the more the better, you know."

"Just let me count," said Diamond, holding up his fingers. "There's Mother first, and then baby, and then me. Next there's old Diamond and the cab — no, I won't count the cab. Then there's that man next door who drinks, and his wife and baby —"

"They're no friends of mine!" said his father.

"Well, they're friends of mine," said Diamond.

"Much good they'll do you!" said his father, laughing.

"I'm sure they will," said Diamond, smiling.

His father stopped laughing suddenly. "Well, go on, Diamond," he said. "Tell me more of *your* friends."

"MUCH GOOD THEY'LL DO YOU!"

"Well, there's Mr. and Mrs. Coleman, and Miss Coleman and Mrs. Crump. And that clergyman who spoke to me one day when the wind had blown down a tree in the Colemans's yard."

"What's his name?" asked his father, curious. "And where does he live?"

"I don't know," said Diamond.

His father laughed again. "Why, Diamond, you're just counting everybody you know. That doesn't make them friends."

"It doesn't? Oh, I thought it did. Well, but then they *will* be my friends."

"And how will that be?"

"Well, they can't help themselves, you know, if I choose to be *their* friend. Oh, yes, then there's that girl, Nanny. Surely she's a friend, anyhow. If it weren't for her, you'd never have got Mrs. and Miss Coleman to ride in our cab."

His father looked at him for a while. "A fine set

"...CAN'T HELP THEMSELVES... IF I CHOOSE TO BE THEIR FRIEND"

of friends you do have, to be sure, Diamond," he said. He was not laughing now, not even smiling.

"Oh, yes," said Diamond happily. "Then there's that new gentleman, Mr. Raymond."

"Yes, if he does what he says," said his father.

Now Diamond looked puzzled. "Why shouldn't he?" he asked. "I bet sixpence isn't too much for him to spare, Father. But I don't understand. Is nobody my friend except the one that does something for me?"

"No, I guess I wouldn't say that, my boy," said his father. "You'd have to leave out baby then."

"Oh, no, I wouldn't! Baby can laugh in your face, and crow in your ears, and make you feel so happy. You wouldn't call that nothing, would you, Father?"

His father looked down at his hands on his knees. Slowly he took the reins, gave them a little twitch, and the cab started rolling. It was early evening and

THE CAB STARTED ROLLING

the sun was orange and low, just peering over the houses along the streets. Time to start home.

"And there's the best of mine to come, and that's you, Father," Diamond said. "And Mother too. You're my friend, Father, aren't you? And I'm your friend, aren't I?"

His father looked at little Diamond's face staring up at him. "And God for us all," his father said softly. His voice broke a little on the last word. He looked ahead again, staring at old Diamond's broad back as the horse clopped lazily down the street.

The old horse knew his way home so well that he didn't have to be led at all. And that was a good thing, because tonight his driver wasn't driving. He just sat on the box, a tear in his eye, his hands slack on the reins, and his thoughts far, far away.

"AND GOD FOR US ALL"

HE DECIDED TO GO SEE MR. RAYMOND

9
Diamond to the Rescue

That very night Diamond's father began to teach him to read. Diamond learned very quickly, because his father used the nursery rhyme book that Diamond and his mother had picked up on the beach.

In only a month Diamond could recognize all the letters and make out words, though slowly and carefully. The rhymes all seemed to be like the one the stream sang at the back of the north wind. At least they sounded like it. Although Diamond enjoyed them very much, his mother and father thought they were nonsense. Diamond often had to explain to his parents what the rhymes meant. One, though, was hard to understand even for him. He decided to go see Mr. Raymond. He had an idea that Mr. Raymond might be able to tell him the meaning of this rhyme.

But one day Diamond had another, more important reason to go see the gentleman.

Diamond had gone with his father on the cab for several days in a row. Each day he noticed that Nanny wasn't at her crossing. On the fourth day, Diamond grew troubled. He came up to the cab just as his father was helping a passenger inside.

"Father, I want to go look after the girl, Nanny," Diamond said. "She must not be well."

"All right," said his father, shutting the cab door. "Just take care, Diamond." He tousled Diamond's hair.

Diamond raced down the street, trying to remember how Nanny had led him to old Sal's that night. It seemed so long ago now. On a corner he asked a policeman for directions, and the policeman pointed out the street.

Diamond was right. Nanny wasn't well. He

DIAMOND RACED DOWN THE STREET

found her at Sal's, lying on a dirty mattress covered with blankets that were little better than rags. Her face was very pale. Her eyes were glazed and staring and her dirty little cheeks were sunken. Sal wasn't home. Nanny didn't move, didn't even seem to know Diamond was there. He had to get help for her, and quickly!

When Diamond reached his father's place by the curb, his father wasn't there. He was probably driving passengers somewhere. Diamond's next thought was Mr. Raymond. Diamond's father had shown him where the gentleman lived, so Diamond ran now to that place.

He was out of breath when he knocked on the door.

"Come in, my little man," said Mr. Raymond. "I suppose you've come to claim your sixpence."

"No, sir, not that," said Diamond, panting.

"What! Can't you read yet?"

HER EYES WERE GLAZED AND STARING

"Yes, I can now, a little. But I'll come for that next time. I came to tell you about Nanny." And Diamond told Mr. Raymond how he had found her.

Mr. Raymond looked alarmed now. He spoke quickly. "Wait right here." He ducked inside and returned with his hat and cane and took Diamond by the hand. "Come with me," he said. "We'll get help for your Nanny."

Mr. Raymond hailed a cab at the next street and sent the driver rushing to the children's hospital, a few blocks away. There Mr. Raymond had a stretcher sent at once to Sal's address to pick up Nanny.

And later that day, washed and dressed in a clean white gown and safely tucked away in a warm clean bed, Nanny slept at the children's hospital. Diamond hardly recognized her as he and Mr. Raymond walked into the big room where all the children stayed.

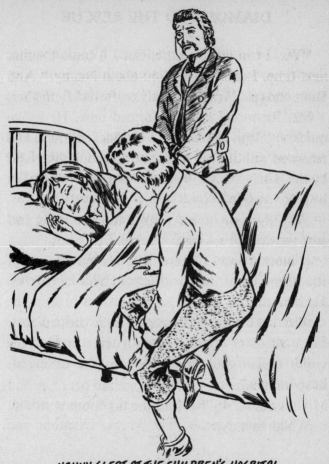

NANNY SLEPT AT THE CHILDREN'S HOSPITAL

But the children recognized Mr. Raymond. Their faces lit up upon seeing him. Soon they were crying, "Give us a story, please! A story, a story!"

He laughed. "All right, children," he said, and sat down on the end of a bed in the middle of the room. The story he told was not one Diamond or any of the other children had ever heard. It was, in fact, Mr. Raymond's own story, one he had just written into a book.

Diamond didn't know it then but Mr. Raymond was a poet and a writer of children's books. He had already written several stories just for the children at the hospital, one of his favorite places. He went there often to read or tell stories to the children. The children of London were among his best friends.

That night Mr. Raymond led Diamond home. When they reached The Mews, Diamond ran

HE LAUGHED...AND SAT DOWN ON THE END OF A BED

inside to ask his mother if he could walk to Mr. Raymond's house with him. She was happy to let him. When Diamond came out again, he was carrying the nursery rhyme book.

"Ah, now you'd like to show me you can read," said Mr. Raymond, smiling. "And you'd like your sixpence."

"No, maybe some other time," said Diamond as they walked. "I wanted you to help me understand a rhyme in this book."

Mr. Raymond took the book. "Perhaps if I read it to you, then you might better understand it," he said. Diamond was happy for that, because it was still hard for him to make out all the words, and it went very slowly for him.

> "Never you mind," said Little Boy Blue;
> "That's what I tell you. If that you won't do,
> "I'll get up at once, and go home without you,
> I think I will; I begin to doubt you."
> He rose; and up rose the snake on its tail,

MR. RAYMOND TOOK THE BOOK

And hissed three times, half a hiss, half a wail.
Little Boy Blue he tried to go past him;
But wherever he turned, sat the snake and faced him.
"If you don't get out of my way," he said,
"I tell you, snake, I will break your head."
The snake he neither would go nor come;
So he hit him hard with the stick of his drum.
The snake fell down as if he were dead,
And Little Boy Blue set his foot on his head.
And all the creatures they marched before him,
And marshalled him home with a high cockolorum.

When Mr. Raymond was finished, Diamond asked, "What do you think it means?"

"Well, I think it means that people may have their way for a while, if they like, but it will get them into such troubles that they'll wish they hadn't had their way."

"I know, I know!" said Diamond. "Like the poor cabman next door to us. He drinks too much."

"WHAT DO YOU THINK IT MEANS?"

"Just so," said Mr. Raymond, nodding. "But when people want to do right, things about them will try to help them. Only they must kill the snake, you know."

"I was sure it had to do with the snake," Diamond said. "That's what I have to do always, kill the snake. Whenever baby cries and won't be happy, and whenever Father and Mother talk about their troubles."

Mr. Raymond looked at Diamond closely. "And how do you do that, my boy?" he asked.

"Oh, I help Mother with her work," Diamond said. "And I make songs for baby. They're awfully silly, but they please baby, and that's all they're meant for."

"Could you let me hear one of them now?"

"No, sir, I couldn't. I forget them as soon as I'm done with them. Besides, I couldn't make a line without baby on my knee. We make them

"AND HOW DO YOU DO THAT, MY BOY?"

together, you know.''

Mr. Raymond was studying Diamond's face, looking deeply into his eyes. He was silent for awhile. When he spoke he was staring beyond Diamond and speaking as if to himself, or as if answering his own thoughts. "I suspect the child's a genius," he said very quietly, "and that's what makes people think he's silly."

But Diamond heard. "What's a genius?" he asked.

His voice seemed to startle Mr. Raymond. "A genius is someone who understands things without anyone telling him what they mean," Mr. Raymond said. "God makes a few every now and then to teach the rest of us."

Diamond frowned. "But I didn't understand the rhyme," he said.

"You understood it well enough when you could hear it for yourself," Mr. Raymond said,

"I SUSPECT THE CHILD'S A GENIUS"

putting his hands on Diamond's shoulders. "But anyway, a genius is not one who understands tricks, but truths."

They had reached Mr. Raymond's house. "Come inside," he said, "and I'll give you your sixpence and your book. It's one I wrote myself."

Later, when Mr. Raymond had walked Diamond home, he put his hand on Diamond's head. The two friends stood for a moment, smiling at each other. Then Mr. Raymond said, "Diamond, please tell your father to come and see me sometime. I wish to speak with him."

"... TELL YOUR FATHER TO COME SEE ME ..."

IT WAS A DREAM COME TRUE FOR DIAMOND'S FAMILY

9
At the Back of the North Wind

I met Diamond at The Mound, Mr. Raymond's new home in the hills of Kent. Mr. Raymond, you see, had married and had moved to a home in the country. And he had asked Diamond's father to come and be his coachman.

It was a dream come true for Diamond's family. They now lived in a beautiful little cottage near the Raymonds's house. In the summer red and white roses bloomed in the rose bushes that climbed up the sides of the cottage. There were beech trees and rolling meadows full of wildflowers. Diamond's father had a nice, clean stable for old Diamond and a new carriage.

And Nanny had come. After she recovered, she stayed with Mr. Raymond. Now in the new home in Kent, she lived with Diamond's family.

She spent most of her time helping Diamond's mother, who was delighted to have a little girl in the house, just like a daughter.

Diamond had become the Raymonds's little page boy. They gave him a blue suit and his own room, high up in one of the dormers. The room had a window that faced the east lawn, which sloped away down into the woods. Diamond said it was the best room in the house. "It's the nearest to the north wind," he said.

And, of course, this made his parents very proud. They didn't mind that he stayed with the Raymonds, because they were right next door and they saw their little Diamond every day.

Mr. Raymond didn't actually use Diamond as a page. He and his wife were just so fond of him that they wanted to be near him as much as they could. Mr. Raymond often put Diamond "to work" by giving him a book to read and asking

DIAMOND HAD BECOME THE RAYMONDS LITTLE PAGE BOY

his opinion of it. Sometimes it would be a book Mr. Raymond had written.

I had known Mr. Raymond for years. When he moved to The Mound we became neighbors, for I lived just down the lane. I began to visit the Raymonds quite often.

And that's how I met Diamond. He was sitting at the foot of a great beech tree a few yards from the lane, reading a book. I saw that the title was *The Little Lady and the Goblin Prince*. It was one Mr. Raymond had written.

After my visit with the Raymonds I walked past the tree on my way down the lane. Diamond wasn't there. But suddenly I stopped. I heard a voice, a soft, childish voice. It seemed to be coming from the top of the tree. I listened, very still.

"What would you see if I took you up to my little nest in the air?" came the sweet voice. "You would see the sky like a clear blue cup turned up-

'I LISTENED...VERY STILL'

side down there.''

"Diamond?'' I called.

"Yes?'' came his voice. "I'm up in my nest.''

"What do you do up there?''

"Oh, I sit and I look at the sky and I make songs.''

"I can't see you,'' I said, straining my eyes to peer up through the thick branches.

"I can't see you either,'' he said, "but I can see the first star peeping out of the sky. I would like to get up into the sky. Don't you think I shall, someday?''

"Yes, I do. Tell me, what else do you see up there?''

"Nothing more, except a few leaves, and the big sky over me. But the wind is like kisses from a big lady. When I get up here I feel as if I am in North Wind's arms.''

That was the first I heard of North Wind. But

'THAT WAS THE FIRST I HEARD OF NORTHWIND'

I would hear much more. Over the weeks that followed, I visited Diamond often. And he told me the story of the North Wind, as I've retold it in this book. Only he told me so much more that I thought I could never write all of it. After all, I thought, who would ever believe it?

Diamond spent a lot of time in his "nest." I would often be returning home after a visit to The Mound and would stop under the beech and listen. From up in the dark, swaying branches, under a deep blue sky sprinkled with the first stars of the evening, I would hear his soft voice, singing his songs.

I asked him where he got his songs. Sometimes he would say, "I made that one." And sometimes he would say, "I don't know. I found it somewhere," or, "I got that one at the back of the north wind."

The little girl, Nanny, was kind enough to

'I WOULD STOP UNDER THE BEECH AND LISTEN'

Diamond, but often she would not play with him. She would tap her forehead, roll her eyes, and say, "He's God's baby. Not quite right, you know."

Diamond would hear her and just smile, and a faraway look would come into his eyes. As for me, I began to wonder if he really were God's baby, a little angel fallen to earth.

Then one day Diamond wasn't up in his nest. Mrs. Raymond, looking somber, said Diamond had taken ill. He was lying in bed upstairs in his little room. I went up to see him.

He was very pale and drawn. But his bright blue eyes were as shiny as ever. He sounded very excited as he told me that North Wind herself had come to him last night. She had taken him outside and they had flown over meadows and forests, he said. And they had raced along a winding stream and listened to the bubbling song it made.

NORTHWIND HERSELF HAD COME TO HIM LAST NIGHT

Then Diamond told me of the things he and North Wind had spoken.

" 'People call me by dreadful names,' " North Wind had said. " 'And they think they know all about me. But they don't. Sometimes they call me Bad Fortune, sometimes Evil Chance, sometimes Ruin, and they have another name for me that they think the most dreadful of all.' "

" 'What is that?' " Diamond had asked.

" 'I won't tell you that name. Do you remember having to go through me to get into the country at my back?' "

" 'Yes! How cold you were, North Wind! And so white, all but your eyes. My heart grew like a lump of ice, and then I forgot for awhile.' "

" 'You were very near knowing what they call me just then,' " North Wind had said. " 'Would you be afraid if you had to go through me again?' "

' "THEY THINK THEY KNOW ALL ABOUT ME... BUT THEY DON'T" '

" 'No, why should I?' " Diamond had said. " 'I would be glad enough just to get another peep at the country at your back.' "

" 'You've never seen that country, Diamond.' "

" 'Haven't I, North Wind? Oh, I thought I had. What did I see, then?' "

" 'Only a picture of it. The real country at my real back is ever so much more beautiful than that. You shall see it one day — perhaps before very long.' "

Diamond fell asleep as he spoke, a peaceful smile on his face. His window was open and a cool breeze came in, playing ever so gently with the golden curl lying on his forehead.

It was a couple of days before I came back. Diamond's mother met me at the Raymonds's door. She was silent, and I could see that she had been weeping. She led me upstairs to Diamond's room.

'I KNEW...HE HAD GONE TO THE BACK OF THE NORTHWIND'

He lay in his little bed, as white as the sheet drawn up to his chin. But his face was beautiful, so peaceful. There indeed lay God's baby, a little angel made of ivory.

I stood there for a long time, gazing at that sweet face. After what seemed like hours, I went downstairs and out into the lane. I stopped by the beech tree. The branches were swaying very gently in the evening breeze. As I looked up at the branches, at the sky, a tear rolled down my cheek. But I smiled to myself and started down the lane.

They said their little Diamond had died. But I knew better. I knew he had only gone to the back of the North Wind.